ABRACA-DOODLE

EVA EVERHARD

ABRACA-DOODLE
Eva Everhard
Copyright 2026 Angels and Fire Books
All Rights Reserved

This book is a work of fiction. Any references to real events, real people, and real places are used fictitiously. Other names, characters, places, and incidents are products of the author's imagination, and any resemblance to persons, living or dead, actual events, organizations, or places is entirely coincidental.
All rights are reserved.
This book is intended for the purchaser only. No part of this book may be reproduced or transmitted in any form or by any means, graphic, electronic, or mechanical, including photocopying, recording, taping, or by any information storage retrieval system, without the express written permission of the author. All songs, song titles, and lyrics contained in this book are the property of the respective songwriters and copyright holders.

ISBN eBook: 978-1-7645213-0-7
ISBN Paperback: 978-1-7645213-1-4
Disclaimer: The material in this book contains sexual content and is intended for mature audiences ages 18 and older.
No generative AI was used in any part of this book.

Book Design by Angels and Fire Books
Cover Design by RJ Creatives
Published by Angels and Fire Books
Cover Image Copyright 2026
All Rights Reserved

Also by Stefanie Dawn

Unearthly Sins Novels
The Demon in Me
The Angel in Her
Lure of a Demon
Dark Angel
Touch of a Demon
The Demon in Him

Elements of Abduction
Savior
Rescuer
Redeemer
Liberator
Releaser
Freer

Standalone Novellas
Demonic
Daemonia

Guardians Trilogy
Rogue Heart
Shattered Heart
Reborn Heart

Hellhound Sins Novels
Curse of a Hellhound

Also by Eva Everhard

Doodle-verse
Doodle Me
Abraca-Doodle

DEDICATION

To anyone who's wanted to shout
FOR THE LOVE OF GOD, JUST SAY COCK
while reading a romance

TRIGGER WARNING

Those who read Doodle Me before this know what the trigger warnings are.

Those who haven't need to very quickly become comfortable with terms like

"custard chucker", "mossy cleft",

and "gentleman's relish"

He has magic hands, and all I can think of as I watch him perform his tricks is how I have a magic ring to show him.

I can make all sorts disappear.

I want his banana in my fruit salad, but when he wants more from the relationship, I'm not sure I'm ready.

Abraca-Doodle is as spicy as it is cringy, with all your least favorite terminologies.
So, pump up that ding-a-ling and prepare your self-saucing taco — Abraca-Doodle is laughably erotic.

WWW.ANGELSANDFIREBOOKS.COM.AU

Contents

1. Chapter One — 1
2. Chapter Two — 19
3. Chapter Three — 34
4. Chapter Four — 53
5. Chapter Five — 72
6. Chapter Six — 79
7. Chapter Seven — 94
8. Chapter Eight — 105
9. Acknowledgements — 111

Chapter One

TINA

There's one thing I always look for in a man—he has to be good with his hands.

And as I watched the hands of the man before me, I was seconds away from fanning myself. Eventually, I gave in to the urge and turned away slightly so I could puff air past my lips and try to cool my heated face, aware of the pink flush on my cheeks.

A magician at a child's party had absolutely no

right being that hot.

My gaze returned to the movement of his hands, and I rubbed my thighs together under my summer dress. A breeze rushed through the garden, and my flaps quivered in happiness, as though they too were excited about the potential of this man's hands. Or maybe they were waving hello, hoping he'd see the brush of movement under the fabric and come to greet us.

God, how long had it been since I'd gotten some good, hard man meat between those lips?

Too long.

They were practically crying out for him, and if I shifted correctly, maybe I could get the wind to play through my channel and call him to me with a soothing baritone.

Sighing, I rubbed my face. It had definitely been too long since I'd had a bit of the ol' in-out in-out, considering the way I was fantasizing about this stranger.

The magician looked up from under his brow, his dark eyes piercing mine. Perhaps he could sense my horniness, or had seen in his peripheral vision the way I'd rubbed my thighs together. Or maybe my lady garden was indeed calling to him on some unspoken level beyond our understanding. My pink fortress may have been able to communicate with him telepathically.

A telepathic pussy.

A telepussy, if you will.

I wanted to say his eyes were limpid pools of loveliness, through which I could see into his very soul, or something equally romantic. But instead, all I could think was how I wanted him to watch me from under that thick, sexy unibrow of his as he coated his hand in my cookies and cream. Maybe he'd lick it off as he watched me with that same look, where it seemed he could see right into the depths of my depraved mind.

When our eyes met, I bit my lip before I grinned at him, and he arched half of his brow.

The sun hit his face, and before he squinted, I realized his eyes weren't brown, but green. A dark green like the waters of an abandoned pond in a backyard, murky and deep, and hiding all sorts of slimy secrets. My squelchy pink zone ached to be one of his slimy secrets.

I rubbed my thighs together again as he finished off his act.

Finish off on me.

The children laughed and cheered, and my nephew, Evan, raced toward his mother, my sister, Lily, and threw his arms around her waist. "Did you see? Did you see?" he asked, in all the high-pitched excitement only a six-year-old could manage.

"I saw," Lily replied with a chuckle, and patted

his head.

Before she could turn to me, I had disappeared from her side, a woman on a mission. I made my way purposefully toward the magician with the magic hands. A hint of guilt stabbed at my side for not engaging with Lily and Evan after the show, but I ignored it. I was drawn to this man, and despite several dancefloor face-sucking events, I hadn't felt a magnetic pull such as this before, and I simply couldn't let it pass.

He was packing up his props, and I cleared my throat as I came to a stop behind him, admiring his buttocks moving in his pants like two dogs play-fighting under a tarpaulin. Shifting and stretching...

Swallowing heavily, I stilled as he turned to face me and straightened to his full height. His eyebrow wiggled enticingly like an ocean wave in a storm as he eyed me. The undulation hypnotized me, and for a moment I was struck speechless, lost in the spell of his tantalizing brow. I licked my lips, my mouth dry.

All the things I could do to this man, and all the things he could do *to me,* raced through my mind.

I wanted him.

Now.

"Hi," I said, and after an awkward pause, I held my hand out. "I'm Tina, Lily's sister."

"Lucas," he crooned, his voice thick like maple syrup, and I wanted to coat myself in it and let him lick it off, leaving trails of shiny saliva as though a snail had slimed across my naked body.

"Great show," I whispered, barely able to muster the strength to talk normally. This man was intoxicating, and his scent filled my nostrils—liquid leather and balloon rubber with a tinge of metal from his magic rings.

I wanted to show him my magic ring. I could

make all sorts disappear.

He smiled, and it only enhanced the effect he had on me. "Thank you," he replied.

"How long have you been doing magic shows?"

Lucas's eyebrow wiggled again as if of its own volition, and I imagined it as a separate entity, staring down at me from his forehead and assessing the conversation as well as my rack. Small talk wasn't my strong suit, but I could feel the daggers of my sister's glare pressing against my back, and while I refused to turn around, I was hoping Lucas and I could chat long enough for her to stop staring. It wouldn't be the first time I'd ditched her somewhere for a man, and I knew I should feel guiltier about that than I did. But at least this time she was at home.

Though I wasn't completely blind to the inappropriateness of trying to pick someone up at my nephew's party, I couldn't resist Lucas.

"A couple of years, but I started doing magic tricks in high school."

"Bet you were popular." Sarcasm slipped through my tone without intent, but my sense of horror had a bucket of water thrown over it when Lucas laughed. My own laugh covered my discomfort. "Sorry, I didn't mean–"

"It's fine."

We looked at each other for a moment, and I tried to assess the whirlwind of sensations moving through my body and figure out what *exactly* it was about him that had me so flustered. This wasn't like me. I saw what I wanted, and I went after it. If I were rejected, no harm, no foul, and I moved on. But it was as though something had literally reached out from him and drawn me across the freshly mowed lawn to his side. Several times, I opened and closed my mouth trying to find the words to ask him what I desperately wanted to, and he watched me with a knowing smile.

Finally, I regained myself and straightened my back, pushing my chest out for him to admire. My nipples tickled the fabric of my dress, swirling playfully, hoping to catch his attention. They successfully caught his eye and pointed toward him in excitement. The sensation ran down my body all the way to my furry mound, and once again I rubbed my thighs together, hoping one of my flaps would catch his attention next. As if on cue, Lucas scanned my body with those frog-wart green eyes before he raised his gaze back to mine.

My horniness was making it hard to think, my entire body almost vibrating with need at his proximity. I needed a good boinking, and I needed it *now*. I wanted his doodle to be the meat in my ham sandwich, and to fill me with his mayonnaise.

"This may be a little forward, but perhaps you'd like to find somewhere quiet so you can... show me a few magic tricks?"

His eyebrow raised again, and I shuddered under the intensity of his gaze. "Won't your sister be upset if you disappear during her son's birthday?"

"We won't be long." I took a step closer to him so we were chest to chest, and shimmied so he could feel the hard lines of my bullet nipples pressing against him. *Pew pew.* "Just a quick private show, then we can get drinks together later, after the party, and see where the night takes us."

Lucas's gaze raked the crowd as the celebration continued behind us, and slowly a grin formed on his face. "Do you have somewhere in mind?"

"I do," I said, and nodded curtly as I swiftly headed toward the house. "Follow me."

He did, and I could feel the heat of him at my

back as I entered the rear sliding doors into the kitchen. I led him around a corner and gestured for him to head into the basement.

He chuckled. "Should I be nervous?"

I rolled my eyes and grinned. "It's a rec room. There's a third bathroom down there. No one will disturb us."

Lucas paused long enough to make another tingle run down my spine at the look he gave me, before he descended the stairs with me behind him, my breasts bouncing boobily. [1]

The moment I closed the door behind us after leading him into the spacious bathroom, Lucas was on me. His lips found mine in a desperate clash of teeth and gums, and he hummed as he gnashed at my mouth. Lucas opened his mouth wide, engulfing my lips entirely. His saliva dripped down my chin, and I groaned as droplets landed

---

1. *I had to include this somewhere. I had no choice.

on my cleavage. Lucas's tongue worked magic of its own against mine, sliding and slipping around the inside of my mouth as though trying to capture my tongue in a game. The wet muscle played with the buildup of our mixed saliva, forcing it to leak out the sides of my mouth. Our bodies pressed together, and the hard line of his stretcher-stick pressed against me.

Without breaking the kiss, I shifted to my toes and rubbed my rounded mound against his rod. My body sang under his ministrations, his fingers wandering up and down my back and my sides, teasing the edges of my jiggling bosom and leaving me gasping for more. I thrust my flange against his python, wanting it to hiss angrily at me and take control. I needed Lucas to know how much I needed him *now*. His fingers continued to tease my body, and while I writhed under the attention, I desperately desired him to begin jousting at my clam. I gasped loudly when he pulled back, and with a grin, he used his finger to scoop up some of the drool from my chin and push it back into my mouth.

"I hope you're better at swallowing my snake spray," he crooned, luridly licking up my left cheek. "Wouldn't want to leave a string of pearls for everyone to see."

"I guess you'll find out later how much I love to choke on a hog," I said, snapping my teeth in the air between us. "But right now, I want that ding-a-ling in my slop hole."

"Let me show you some magic, baby."

He stepped back, and my brow furrowed as he reached into his pocket and pulled out a long, thin balloon. I watched with a frown as he blew it up, his eyes never leaving mine. His lips were still surrounded by spit, and spittle slapped around the mouth of the balloon, making it flap and quiver.

A squeak escaped the edge of the balloon, and he paused to grin at me.

"Can you make my front butt talk like that, too?" I whispered, my body keening and practically begging him to touch me again. "Can you fuck a queef out of me?"

My flaps quivered in time with the balloon, and I resisted the urge to cup my muffin to try to still the motion. Desperation clawed through my body. I needed this man more than I'd ever needed anyone, and I imagined him shoving his face between my legs and blowing raspberries against my mossy cleft.

I couldn't have imagined that watching a man blow up a balloon could be so erotic, but as it rose between us, the purple tip stretching to accommodate the air forced into it, I bit my lip as I held back a moan. Lucas deftly tied the end off and stood before me, holding the balloon near his crotch and waving it slowly from side to side.

"Do you want my doodle in your meat sleeve? Is your pastrami sandwich desperate for some attention, hmm?" he asked, and I nodded frantically. "Then remove your panties and spread those legs."

With trembling fingers, I did as he asked. Need surged through me, and my pink parts inflamed with desire. My flange lips became puffy with need, and Lucas looked down and admired my rounded mound, like a ripe peach, as I lifted my dress to show him more. When I spread my legs, my musky, savory scent filled the bathroom, and Lucas's nostrils flared wide like two tunnels on a freeway as he took it in—cured meats and umami flavor, all rolled together in my gooey wetness, ready for him.

Lucas lowered the balloon, and I gasped. "Oh my!" My eyes widened as he positioned it between my legs. "Are you going to..."

"Yes," he said, and gave me a dazzling smile before he pushed the head of the balloon against my flower. My flaps parted for him, welcoming the intrusion, and closed delicately over the balloon as it penetrated me, like flower petals closing once the sun had disappeared. My eyes rolled back as my juicy nectar dripped down the balloon, and the squeeze of his wet hand against the rubber only made the situation even more erotic.

"Oh... Lucas..." I moaned and tried to stay still as he fucked me gently with the balloon, the sound reminiscent of moving a plastic straw in and out of a takeaway cup.

Squeak squeak squeak.

Squeak squeak squeak.

"I need to warn you, Tina," he said with a low growl, and I forced my eyes to open and meet his gaze. "I don't make love... I make magic." I gasped as he slid the balloon out of me, and my lady parts flapped around angrily at the loss. He watched the motion with amusement. "Looks like I made her upset."

"Well, you'd better fix it, or we'll *both* be upset."

He nibbled the end of the balloon and hummed with satisfaction at my musky flavor. His teeth nicked the rubber, and with a loud raspberry, the balloon flew out of his hand and rocketed around the room. We both followed the motion with our gazes until it stopped and landed in the tub, and Lucas turned to me with a grin. "Let's see if I can make that grassy knoll talk the same way."

"Oh, please..."

"Don't worry, baby, I've got what you need right here." Lucas unbuttoned the large brass buttons of his fly and pulled his hot-rod out of his pants. It was a glorious cock, and my mouth salivated at the sight of it. Thick and long, with veins that ran up the sides and under the head, making a tapestry designed for my pleasure. His balls were heavy and jiggled as he rubbed his fuck-pole in his palm. I wanted to suck on them, to draw one into my mouth and roll it around like a gobstopper. I wanted to floss my teeth on the hair on his sack.

"Next time, I want you naked," Lucas said as I drew my gaze from his mini-boulders to his eyes. "But right now..." He came in close and pressed one hand against the wall, the other running under my dress and cupping my ass. "I'm going to bludgeon your piss flaps. Hard and dirty."

Chapter Two

Lucas

It's not a bad gig, working in entertainment. The agency I'm signed with keeps me busy, and I do most things—from being a magician or a clown, to Santa or a mascot. It was fun, the kids loved it, and I had fairly flexible hours and many, many interesting stories.

But not *one* of my past experiences since I'd joined the agency six years ago could have prepared me to find a drop-dead-gorgeous woman at a party, single, and ready to get down and do the bang-bang. Who wanted me *so* desperately that she didn't ask me out on a date. No. Instead, she all but dragged me to a downstairs bathroom and demanded I give her a clunge-plunge.

"Just dick me already!" Tina cried out, and with a grin, I obliged.

Lifting her against the wall, I dipped the tip of my drill into her oil well. She was so wet, so turned on and ready for me that my fuck-stick slid right into her waiting cavern. Tina's body stretched to accommodate me, and her moans were so pretty as I pierced her. Slapping a hand over her mouth, I shushed her. "Better keep quiet, sugar plum, we wouldn't want anyone to hear us." She murmured something against my hand, but I kept it over her mouth as I pile-drove into her, slamming her luscious butt-cheeks against the cool wall with each thrust. One of her legs dropped slightly, but we made do, and from the way her eyes rolled back—so far they almost rolled over again—it didn't seem as though she were complaining about the position.

"There are so many things I want to do to you," I murmured against her ear, taking the lobe between my teeth and grazing it. Tina moaned against my palm as I continued doodle-bopping her. "I'm going to gargle that oyster of yours, gonna lap up all your sweet salty juices. My tongue is going to be so dry from licking you so much it'll be like sandpaper up your slit, but you'll love it anyway." Tina nodded frantically, and I chuckled. "I want you to ride my face so hard, my goatee will be completely mopped in your vulva juices. I want that scent on me. I want to have prawn breath for hours. I want to smell like a seafood dinner so I can think of how delicious you are all damn day and night."

Tina turned her head to the side, and I released her mouth. Her heated gaze fell upon me. "Do I get to gargle you? Do I get to suck you so hard my mouth fills with your gentlemen's relish and I can hold it in my mouth and savor it?" My mouth went dry, and I swallowed. Dirty talk with this woman was like a challenge. Who could rile the other one up more? Pounding into her hole, with the slurping and slopping sounds and the sheer ache from how hard my prick was, it seemed we were both winning. "Maybe I won't swallow..." Tina continued with a smirk. "Maybe I'll keep it in my mouth until the relish becomes chowder, and I can get a decent meal from it and chew it before it slides down my slutty throat."

"Oh, you are such a slut, aren't you?" I panted out.

How did I get so lucky to find this woman?

"I'll be a slut for you. I want your porn syrup all

over me."

"Oh, fiddlesticks," I muttered, my voice breaking as she hummed. "I'm going to…"

"Do it. Let your doodle spew into me. Fill me with your spooge."

"Shut up and kiss my mouth hole." I swallowed her answering moan, and it mingled with mine as I enclosed my mouth around hers, wide and waiting for me to plunge my flavor muscle into. My peak came then, and my knees weakened as my body jerked and stuttered through my pleasure-haze. Tina moaned against my lips, vibrating them with the sound and sending waves of pleasure through me as my entire body shook. My man-meat jolted up into her in quick shunting thrusts as I emptied the gooey gravy from my balls into her waiting tunnel. Tina's orgasm followed shortly after, and she flailed against the wall like a fish out of water as wave after wave of electric pleasure pulsed through her.

We stayed like that, panting for a few minutes, slumped against each other and sharing the same air.

"Oh my God..." she muttered, her lips pressed against my shoulder. "That was so good. Your pickle is incredible."

"My pickle was a bit nervous."

"Was it? It didn't show."

Leaning back, I smiled at her and cupped her face in my hands. Her cheeks were flushed a shade of pink that reminded me of flowers in springtime, or perhaps of the shade the head of my spurtle-stick goes after a vigorous wank. "You're so beautiful."

Her eyes narrowed even as she smiled. "Are you free tonight?"

My smile faltered, and the nervousness in my pickle returned, and it sagged against my leg, leaving a trail of goop on my thigh. Tina intrigued me, and while our bang-bang session had been incredible, I wanted to get to know her better.

I wanted to *date* and to become more than just a physical release.

But was that what she wanted?

Smiling widely, I pressed my lips to hers, our kiss like four hotdog sausages pressed together, their rounded edges meeting. "Yes, of course. What do you have in mind?"

She grinned. "I know a place."

The place she had in mind turned out to be a nightclub, and while it had been a stretch since I'd gone clubbing, I was up for it. It was only a few hours after the party had finished that I met Tina outside the venue. Tina's sister had glared at her heavily as she'd spied us returning to the party, and I was thankful my jeans were dark so the wet patch her pussy yoghurt had left on my thigh and crotch weren't as noticeable. The way Lily had stared hard at Tina made me wonder if this was a regular occurrence for her. If she threw herself at every man she was attracted to and parted her legs, revealing her panty hamster for the taking for anyone and everyone.

I had no issue with it if that were the case. Tina's sexual history was her own business, and if she was happy, then I couldn't care less.

What I *did* care about, however, was the spurring of feelings that seemed to be growing in my chest the more time I spent with her. A quick frickle-frackle in a bathroom may have been all she was after. Maybe she wanted more fun time tonight—and I was more than up for it—but with each passing hour, the window for me to casually find out if she was after *more* felt as though it were closing. Soon, it would be *assumed* I knew where we stood, and if she stood firmly on the line of getting her canoe waxed and nothing more, then I would be that man.

But I needed to know, because if she wanted more, my tallywacker would stand to attention and practically bounce around in my pants in excitement. Because *I* wanted more. I wanted to come home to this woman every night. I wanted to plough her goddamn field. I wanted to go balls deep, fishing in her deep sea. I wanted her poop-button on my tongue. I wanted it *all* with her.

I grew up on a farm, and when I was a teenager, my cousin told me sex was like doing it with the pulp of a freshly picked pumpkin, still warm from the sun. I tried it, but it didn't really work because he had already used it, and the premade tunnel offered little sensation. Then I got a seed stuck in the end of my urethra, but I was too scared to go to the doctors and tell them what I'd done, so I waited until I needed to pee and then forced it out until it *pinged* on the porcelain of the toilet.

Anyway, sex with Tina was like, totally, way better than that.

We'd been chatting and drinking for an hour, maybe two. Time seemed to have no meaning in this woman's company. Clearing my throat, I opened my mouth to ask her if she wanted to *date,* when Tina turned to me with a grin and said, "Do you want to dance?"

My jaw snapped shut, and my gaze wandered to the dancefloor before returning to her. She was bouncing slightly on her heels, her cocktail sloshing in the glass she held.

The moment to ask had passed, and I cursed myself inwardly for not asking earlier in the night.

While we'd been chatting, we'd even touched briefly on past relationships. My opportunity to ask her what she wanted from *us* was *right there*, and I had missed it.

"Of course," I replied with a smile, and Tina grinned before she downed the rest of her cocktail. I watched her throat work around the liquid, and I swallowed, too, unable to get the image of her on her knees, worshiping my sausage before swallowing my sauce, from my mind.

Thankfully, Tina distracted me by grabbing my hand, and we made our way to the dancefloor. Immediately, she pushed her body against mine, her breasts two perfect oblate spheroid melons pressing against the fabric of her tight dress. Her ass cheeks were two ripe apples, undulating as she moved against me. I wrapped my arms around her body, pulled her closer, and pushed my thigh between hers. Tina ground on me, and with my grip on her cheeks, I encouraged her to. I wanted her to drip her thick cream through her panties and dollop it onto my leg. I wanted her to mark me.

Her body was a delicious fruit salad of sensations, and I wanted to explore every nook and cranny.

"Is that a cucumber in your pocket, or are you just happy to see me?" Tina asked next to my ear.

"It's a cucumber."

"Oh."

With a grin, I pulled it from my pocket. "Never know when you're going to get snacky on the dancefloor."

Sliding it into my mouth, I then pulled it back, pressing my front teeth into it and curling two ribbons of cucumber skin from the top. Tina watched the motion with wide eyes, both of us still swaying to the music, and she rubbed herself harder against me. I could feel the nub of her clitoris against my leg, like a plump cherry ready to burst, rounded and ripened and simply waiting to be tasted. The music pounded against our eardrums as I held the cucumber before her lips, and slowly she parted them, and I pushed the vegetable into her mouth.

The way her eyes fluttered closed told me she wasn't thinking about the cucumber. She was imagining my twinkie instead. Much sweeter and certainly not as good for you.

There's no Vitamin K in my pants, only Vitamin D.

When I pulled the cucumber from her mouth with a *pop*, she hummed. People were staring at us, but we didn't care. There was a fiery passion between us, fiery and passionate, like a fiery passion.

I slid the cucumber back into my pocket—in

case I got snacky later—and we continued to dance. Each song blended into the next, and our bodies moved as one. More than once, our eye contact lingered until our eyes watered, because we didn't want to blink. I didn't want to miss a second of how absolutely gorgeous she looked. Her strawberry blonde hair tumbled over her shoulders, precisely the way strawberries wouldn't, and her raspberry lips curved at me when she noticed me looking. Coupled with her milky skin, her entire head was a berry milkshake, and I wanted to lick every inch of her from her forehead to her toenails.

If only I weren't lactose intolerant.

Tina pressed her forehead to mine, and after another two songs, sweat glistened on our skin. My head slipped from hers, and I had to regain myself. She giggled and pressed her palm to my cheek before her lips met mine.

It was magic. Better than the fake magic I made with cheap props. It was *real.*

I wanted this woman. The sparks had gone off and lit the fireworks of desire within me. But it was more than desire, yet I dared not even think it to myself, because it was too soon to be falling for this woman.

"Want to get out of here?" she said, nodding her head toward the exit.

I smiled, even as conflict tore at my chest. "Anything you want, baby cakes."

Her grin was enough to keep the smile on my face as we left the club, but inside I had resolved not to ask her what she wanted from this relationship, if that's even what it was destined to be.

At least not to ask her tonight.

Because if all she wanted were physical, I'd rather that than not have her at all.

Chapter Three

Lucas

Tonight was not the time for thinking.

Those thoughts of uncertainty and *what if*, of wondering what she wanted from *us*, I had locked away. Because as I followed Tina up the stairs to her apartment, I was mesmerized by the movement of those delicious cheeks under her dress. If I dropped back a few steps, I could see the shape of her taco through her panties. The spider legs of her pubic hair crept out of the sides of the fabric, and I licked my lips. I wanted to muff-dive into that large mound and gobble up everything she had to offer.

If I wasn't still finding pubes stuck in my teeth a week later, then I hadn't done my job properly.

The front door closed behind us with a click, and after Tina had locked it, we turned to each other and stared with heated desire flowing through our veins. Her body called to mine, and mine to hers, but instead of rushing at each other as we had earlier today, we lingered and saturated ourselves in the *waiting*. Both denying ourselves what we really wanted, and letting our bodies get worked up.

"Would you like a drink?" she asked, breaking the spell and taking a step closer to me.

"No, thank you." I played her game and took a single step toward her.

We matched each other's movements and

approached one small step at a time until we were mere inches apart. The light in her apartment was crisper than the mood lighting of the club, and the bright yellow of the cheap supermarket bulb played off the colors in her hair. Her brown eyes stared up at me, like chocolate pools I could dip the many fruits I had thought of earlier into. Tina was the complete package, funny and bold, with all the creamy pulpy goodness to match the sexy, fruity shapes of her body, and now liquid chocolate eyes.

She was perfect.

"You turn me on so much," I said quietly. The only other sound in the apartment was the radio on low.

"Tonight, we can do everything." Her words were a passionate promise, and while my mind was still struggling to compute all the options she had held open for me, she dropped to her knees, and my ability to form a coherent thought fizzled out into nothing.

Expertly, she flicked open my belt and undid my pants before she shoved them down to my ankles. Tina smirked when she placed her fingers on the elastic of my boxers. "Cute," she muttered, taking in the magician hat pattern of them before those, too, were discarded to the pile around my ankles.

My python stood to attention and bobbed in her heavy gaze.

"I didn't get much of a chance to admire this earlier," she whispered as she traced a finger delicately up my shaft. "This weewee is a weapon, isn't it?"

"Made for pleasure," I purred, and she laughed.

"Can I taste you?"

I swallowed, and nodded, and Tina parted her lips and stuck out her pink tongue. Her flavor muscle poked and dabbed at the tip of my trouser snake, and the hole at the head of my doodle opened up for her, like a snake unhinging its jaw, and welcomed her, ready to clamp down on her tongue. Tina hummed as she flicked her tongue over and then inside the tip, making out with my snake. When she gripped my shaft and took the fireman's helmet in her mouth, the teasing ended, and Tina sucked and slurped on my fuckstick until I had to steady myself. She hummed and glugged as though she were enjoying a bowl of warm soup. When she went to pull back, I grabbed the back of her head.

"Don't swallow that spit," I said, gripping her hair. "Let it dribble." Tina smiled around my carnal stump, and the drool leaked out of the sides of her mouth and down her chin. "That's it, I like it sloppy." Pulling back, I then thrust into her waiting mouth, and more saliva spilled out past her lips. But she let it, and gobbled my pork down as I slammed into her.

"Open wide," I said as I pulled her off my pipe. "Open up for Mr. Chunky."

Tina gasped as I pushed forward again, all the way in, until my pubic hair tickled her nostrils as my pole sampled the sensations at the back of her throat. She slobbered on my knob so well, and I didn't want to finish, but Mr. Winky couldn't hold out much longer, and the way she was sucking and smacking her lips around my bonophone was too much.

"That's it." I could barely get the words out, and gasped as my high came pushing against my balls. My doodle-berries tightened as I tried to hold back, but it was too strong. "That's it, baby, get ready to swallow my wang pus."

I groaned loudly as thick tadpoles of my semen pushed through my hole and into the warmth of her mouth and throat. Holding Tina's hair,

I made sure she lapped up every drop of my gravy and swallowed it before I pulled back. She gasped loudly before she hummed and ran a finger delicately over her lips.

"Mmmm, your repopulation paste is delicious. Like a thick penis colada."

Bending down, I grabbed her chin and guided her to stand. "My turn to taste you."

"I hope I didn't wear you out," Tina said as she giggled and guided me toward the bedroom, and I followed, waddling like a penguin with my pants around my ankles, feeling as sexy as I looked, which was a lot of sexy. "You better be ready to fill me with your knob slurry tonight."

"Oh, I will, sweet cheeks." She giggled again as I slapped her ass. "You said we can do everything tonight. I wonder if that means you'll open your fart hole for me." I almost choked at the look she gave me, sultry and seductive, as though that was *exactly* what she had planned. "Oh, blimey," I muttered under my breath.

Tina moved to the edge of the bed, and when she grabbed the straps on her dress, I touched her hand. "Please, allow me."

She hummed again. "Use those magic fingers on me."

"I'll use my magic tongue, too."

Her dress came away from her body in a flurry of fabric, sweeping down and over her curves as though made of silk. The silky fabric was so like silk, if I didn't know better, I'd say it was silk. But I did know better, and it wasn't. The more of her milky skin that was exposed to me, the harder I had to work to control myself. This woman was nothing short of a goddess, and every move she made, no matter how subtle, made me want to fall to my knees and worship her. My sugar-lumps were talking to my candy stick, and I grabbed myself and rubbed, needing some friction to halt the runaway train of thoughts in my mind as her body was exposed.

The mounds of her breasts were like two kittens playing underneath the thin material of her bra, and I wondered if they'd want to play with the ferret in my pants. I could lay her down and kneel over her and slide my pecker between those large mounds, squishing them and molding them in my palms. Tina was so open with her body and her sexuality, I really believed she would be up for anything I suggested. No part of her was off limits, it seemed, and I couldn't formulate a coherent thought as too many ideas tumbled over one another in my mind. It didn't help that all the blood was rushing from my brain right to my noodle.

With a sly eyebrow raised, she reached behind her and undid her bra, freeing her gelatinous bosom for me to see. I groaned at the sight of her taut nipples, two pink eyes staring me down in tandem with her brown eyes. Not her butthole, I meant the brown eyes on her face stared at me.

She held a knowing look, and it wasn't a stretch to realize she *knew* how utterly gorgeous she was.

I was in awe of this woman, and while confidence spewed from me the way my man oil spewed from my weenie, my outward confidence was mostly a façade. The same face I put on to perform for crowds could be used in my social life, and from the moment this scrumptious woman approached me and boldly made her intentions clear, my mask was on.

Did Tina want to see my softer side? Was she interested in my squishy innards of emotional vulnerability?

Her panties followed her dress in the tantalizing journey down her silky, milky, creamy, dreamy legs into a pool by her feet, and I let out a breath I didn't know I was holding. Tina had taken over the undressing even after my offer to do it for her. Once I became struck by the sheer dazzling brightness of her beauty, as though a spotlight had shone upon her and all other light sources had been extinguished, she glowed before me, a goddess without a clamshell to stand in.

"Please," I begged, licking my spongey lips. "I need to taste your fur burger."

Tina sat on the edge of the bed and beckoned with her finger before she lay back. "Then come here, big boy." Her legs spread, and I dropped to my knees in worship of her body. Her hot box radiated heat, and I couldn't wait to taste the delicious sticky cookies she had baking in that oven. Tina's moan was so sweet as I spread the lips of her hair pie with my fingers and leaned in to inhale deeply. There was no rush. I could take my time, and though her thighs clamped around my shoulders and she whined and shimmied on the sheets, desperate for attention, I wouldn't be rushed. She looked down over her body, her eyes barely peeking over the tips of her generous bosom, like a frog peering over the surface of a lake, and I grinned at her.

It was her turn to beg. "Please," she whispered.

"This crumper is mine, Tina," I crooned, and blew cool air at her flaps, making them quiver. "I will take my time lapping at this clam." I growled at her badger, and when it growled back, I laughed and soothed it by patting the furry mound. "Patience."

Working her with my fingers, her pink lips opened, unfurling like a flower. Layers upon layers of delicate petals of flesh opened and revealed her to me. Tina's body trembled as her love button came into view, peeking out between the foliage as though it wasn't sure of this intruder. I hummed deep in my throat, a soothing sound to calm her concerned fuzzy wookie. A sharp gasp left Tina's face lips as her twat lips followed suit and folded back for me, and I blew cold air against her bud of pleasure. Another tremble worked through her body. She was on the edge of her peak from this alone, and I marveled at how turned on this woman was for me.

She was mine.

When I tickled the slip-and-slide of her channel with the tip of my finger, her button rippled with pleasure, and as the last petal unfurled fully, I slurped at it with my meaty tongue. Tina cried out, and I let the texture of my erect taste buds work through the layers of her flappy skin, sucking on each individual lip and French kissing her ham sandwich, one slice at a time. Returning my attention to her bud, I swirled my tongue around it expertly, groaning at every sound she released as her pleasure increased. Her peak came faster than I think she was expecting, and her gasps became louder before they morphed into pants. But I didn't stop, and when I slid a finger into her sloppy hole with a squelch, she cried out my name as she came. Her beaver closed around my finger, trying to build a dam and keep me inside her, and I chuckled against her as I lapped up all the creamy goodness she offered me.

Tina was still trembling as I removed my clothes and crawled over her, and with some encouragement, she shuffled upward toward the pillows and sighed loudly as she rested back. Her eyes opened, and she blinked up at me, her orbs staring at me, full of heat and contentment. Reaching down, I pumped my love rocket a few times in my fist, but I was already hard. My aching peg had been rock-hard since the moment we'd entered her apartment, and even as I squirted my thick, goopy juices down her throat, it hadn't eased.

I needed her, and only her muff would do.

"Oh, Lucas," she sighed, and shifted so her legs were parted wider for me. "You're so fucking good. Please, I need you now."

How could I deny this woman the jiffy-stiffing she was begging for? I guided my loaded pipe into her tunnel and pushed forward with one deep thrust. Her hole was already wet from the drizzle of her fish dip, and she took me easily, sliding all the way in until I was as deep as I could go. But I pushed in harder, into her guts, jostling them around. My dinkle was primed and ready to give her the diddling of a lifetime, and her organs shifted to the sides to make room for my giant stick of salami, welcoming me and embracing me as though I were part of her body and not an intruder. Her womb called to me, her ovaries harmonized a backup to the song her body sang, and only one of them couldn't hold a tune.

Eeeeeeeeeeeeeeeeee.

EeeeeeeEEEEEEEeeeeeeee.

Oooooooohhyaaaaaaaaaaeeeeeeee!

The holy music washed over me as our bodies became one. Tina's body responded on an entirely new plane of pleasure, and she started to tremble with an impending release, brought on by the jostling and jamming I was giving her wide-open hole. Her legs parted impossibly far, and her eyes widened like dinner plates, those big orbs staring into my soul as an orgasm tore through her body at frightening speed and intensity. All of her flaps closed around my lollipop like something out of a sci-fi movie, and I groaned at the extra sensation of all the additional layers I had to push through to reach the depth of her heated core. I pounded into her, the bed frame smashing against the wall with such force that plaster dust fell around us. My diglet was ready to release its load of nobslurry, and Tina felt the change in my boner as it thickened inside her, ready to fill her up with all the daddy sauce my cum-chimes no longer had the capacity to hold.

"Are you ready for my bonk-juice, baby?"

"Yes, yes! Let your cock-beans empty deep into my flesh purse!"

"Here it comes!"

Tina cried out, and I roared as my thunderstick unloaded inside her, wave after wave of buttermilk spewed forth from the tip and filled her up, her love bucket taking everything I had to give.

Tina's head lolled side to side as her fuck-wagon stretched to accommodate my load. "Oh me, oh my, oh goodness! Oh, deary me. What a lot of spunk oil you have for me. I can't take it. Oh, but

I must take it. My hollow calls for you to fill it. Yes, God yes!"

The pleasure was all-consuming, and for a moment, all I could see was a bright, white light as my vision faded and then brightened. Her satchel was filled with my syrup, and it milked every last drop from me. Her hoohaa worked around my ding-dong like fingers around the teats of a cow, milking and milking until surely there must be nothing left inside me, and the next time I came it would only be a spurt of dust.

Collapsing on top of Tina, her poontang continued to spasm around me as I kissed her neck. Tina ran her fingers through my hair and kissed my temple in return. Her flange released my cum onto the sheets with a sound like a whoopee cushion being used underwater, and we relaxed into each other's embrace. The feel of her soft mounds and the hard tips of her nipples pressing against me was enough for my tool to start to harden and come to life again.

I would take tonight, and have Tina as many times and in as many different ways as she would let me.

I already knew this woman would ruin me.

Chapter Four

Tina

When I was woken by the sunlight streaming through the window, I groaned and rolled over, only to slap into Lucas's back. This drew a groan from him, and when he rolled over, both the hair on his head and his usually well-groomed brow were disheveled.

I smiled. "Good morning."

He returned my smile. "Good morning, beautiful."

A wistful note of air left my nose as I stared into the ripe-avocado green of his eyes. I couldn't remember the last time I had woken with a man in my bed, and more to the point, the last time I had woken to a man in my bed who I wasn't itching to get the fuck out of my apartment. After our romp last night, I had expected my unexplained infatuation and lust for this man to be dulled. But the throb in my chest and between my legs remained, and I took a moment to stare at him, as if hoping it would go away.

If anything, it increased.

Desire thrummed as my panty-hamster came to life, rolling around joyfully in my underwear.

Lucas's brow furrowed slightly before his face relaxed. It seemed he was assessing me as much as I was him. Much to the disgruntlement of my sister and parents, I wasn't the relationship type, and my history consisted of several flings, the longest lasting four months. My lip twisted slightly. Perhaps I should tell Lucas that before he started looking into things too much.

But *was* he looking into things too much?

Because here he was, in my bed after our night out together and a vigorous rearranging of my organs, and I wanted him to stay. Before I could stop myself, I asked, "Do you want to do something together today?" His eyebrow shot up, and I cleared my throat. "I mean, it's Sunday, I assumed you had the day off, but if you're busy–"

"I'm not busy."

"Well, okay then."

We stared at each other for a beat longer.

"Do you want the first shower?" he asked.

All at once, I was aware of the stank in the room and on my skin. The scent of our boot-knocking sessions lingered in the room, and I shifted, fully aware of the sticky mess between my legs from

Lucas's deep-diving in my crab fishing zone.

"Unless..." Lucas shuffled across the bed until his face was close to mine, and my eyes crossed as I tried to maintain eye contact. "Unless you want me to burp my worm in your corn hole again?"

My eyes glazed over with lust, and Lucas's eyelids became heavy with desire as heat permeated between us. He shuffled closer still, and, remaining on our sides, I lifted my leg and draped it over his thigh. The fragrance of my clam jelly oozed from my pink fortress, and his nostrils flared as he wrapped an arm around me and guided his custard-launcher inside me. The slick sound of his length sinking into my sopping fuckhole had us both moaning, and our combined baby batter oozed out and between my thighs, thoroughly coating his gobstoppers.

We took our time, his thrusts deep and steady, batter-dipping his corn dog slowly. This was the closest I'd ever come to making love, and we held eye contact, both focusing on the sucking and squelching sounds of our genitalia smashing together and our glue mixing and oozing and frothing.

A sensation stabbed at my chest as I stared into the basil pesto green of his orbs, a feeling I knew I could identify if I dared put words to it, but I'd rather not think about it, so I pushed it aside.

To distract myself, I kissed him, sliding my slimy, morning-breath tongue around his. Our teeth clashed as he thrust harder, and I let myself get lost in the moment, ignoring the fear that this man could ruin me.

We'd showered together and almost managed to get through the shower without distraction.

Almost.

But it was impossible.

Lucas and I had soaped each other up, and the time that should have been full of chatting and playful banter was instead filled with intense staring as our hands roamed each other's bodies. My hands were filled with gel-soap when I started giving him a hand job, and the sound of jostling a cocktail shaker in a slime-bath echoed off the shower walls. Before he finished, I dropped to my knees and took his sparkling clean lizard in my mouth. Lucas moaned loudly as I played him like a flute, pressing my teeth into his shaft and head, bouncing my molars off the squishy texture of him. I pulled back as he finished, and let him spray his man period over my face. His spooge expanded like foam, and I relished the bubbly sensation of it on my skin before allowing the shower spray to wash it off.

Lucas had looked down at me as though I were a goddess, and it was intoxicating.

His eyes followed my movement as I drizzled honey on my toast, and he ate his own, offering me a sly look. I giggled. "Keep it in your pants. I need to recover."

"*You* need to recover?" he asked incredulously with a laugh. "You've sucked every last drop of my yogurt from me. *I* need time to recover."

Grinning at him, I bit into my toast. The way he spoke and looked at me felt like worship on some level. I couldn't help but wonder if this was what being with someone was *meant* to feel like. My previous partners had been using me for cave-diving as much as I had been using them. Interactions outside the bedroom were basically two strangers trying to maintain a conversation when they had nothing in common and no real desire to talk to each other. Going on dates felt like roleplay, and it was only when we were in bed that I felt alive.

But that *alive* feeling continued with Lucas even as we sat here eating breakfast.

"So, what did you have in mind for today?" he asked between mouthfuls.

Lifting a shoulder nonchalantly, I responded, "I'm not sure, really."

Something in his algae-green eyes sparkled. "I have an idea, if you're up for a game."

"Sure." I couldn't help the smile that lit my face. This man was intoxicating in the best of ways, and my subconscious was raging. Part of me wanted to find flaws, so I could cling to them and have a reason to kick him to the curb. The other, and arguably bigger, part of me wanted to see this through and follow it wherever it went, as long as it meant spending more time with him.

We finished breakfast and went to my car, as

Lucas had caught a cab to the club last night and we'd ended up back at my place. The clothes he'd worn last night were nice, but suitably casual that we could hang out today. A faint scent of smoke from the club lingered on the fabric as he slid into the passenger seat, and I started the car.

"So, where to?"

"Do you know the Get-Your-Jollies park?"

My brow furrowed. "Yes..."

Lucas smiled. "Do you like mini-golf?"

"I do..."

"But you've never played it the way I do. Head there."

Curiosity piqued, I pulled into the slow-moving Sunday traffic. My cell connected to my car's Bluetooth, and Lucas let out a delighted sound as the playlist popped up on the small screen.

"Oh ho, what do we have here? You can tell a lot about a person from their playlist."

I smiled as I glanced at him, where he poked at the touchscreen, scrolling through my music choices. "Oh yeah? Like what?"

"Like what sort of music someone enjoys."

Silence ebbed through the car, and I glanced at Lucas again. "And?"

"That's it."

"You worked that up like you were going to make a list."

"Nope."

"Okay."

We fell into easy conversation. Lucas told me about his work with the entertainment agency, and I made the obligatory joke about him being a stripper. He laughed and gave me a look full of secrets.

What have we here indeed?

The more layers I pulled back from this man, the more I wanted to know about him. He was carefree and easy-going, but every time he'd make a joke or a quip, he'd glance at me as if to make sure I found it funny. It felt less like he was saying things for him to appear amusing or witty, and more like he genuinely wanted me to have a good time. It was refreshing, and I found myself smiling almost constantly as we neared our destination.

Despite my protests, Lucas paid for the game and handed me my undersized golf club as the dispenser spat out two fluorescent balls. We stepped onto the mini-golf course, and I sucked in a deep, slow breath. The sun was out, but the air was crisp and light. Turning, I found Lucas staring at me, and when I met his gaze, he stepped forward and brushed a lock of hair behind my ear.

"You're truly beautiful, Tina." When I said nothing, he smiled at me, and hesitantly, I returned his smile. Every passing moment with Lucas was increasing that feeling within my chest that I tried desperately to ignore. I barely knew him, and it seemed much too soon for feelings of any sort to be developing. Internally, I could feel myself pulling away, and had to force myself to remain present in the moment.

Just enjoy the date.

"So, what's this special way of playing mini-golf?"

Lucas reached into his pocket, and when he pulled his hand out, he unfurled his fingers to reveal three dice.

My brow furrowed again. "Dice?"

Lucas's eyes glinted with mischief. "Dice. Follow me."

We stood at the first hole, and I placed my yellow ball at the designated spot. Before I could line my club up, Lucas wrapped his hand around mine. "Wait, you don't know the rules yet."

It was impossible not to smile. There was an

energy about him. "Tell me."

He held one of the dies between two fingers. "For the first six holes, we roll the dice before each shot. Whatever number it lands on is the hole you've got to aim for."

I laughed. "Are you serious?"

"Absolutely. We move through the holes chronologically, but each time, you don't know where you'll be aiming until you get there. You're at hole one, but if the dice says three, you gotta aim…" Lucas took a moment to scan the mini-golf course. "There."

I followed where he pointed. Hole three was curved around, and I would have to get the ball not only over hole two entirely, but across a small decorative river with a little wooden bridge. Laughing again, I looked between him and the course. "You're serious, aren't you?"

"Absolutely." Lucas grinned.

"So, the other two dice are for…"

"Holes seven to twelve, and thirteen to eighteen."

"I get it. We'll never be aiming for hole eighteen from hole one."

"Na, gotta set some boundaries. Besides, eventually we're going to draw attention to ourselves. It's best to delay that as much as possible."

I pressed the back of my hand against my lips. "We're going to get kicked out, aren't we?"

"Probably." Before I could argue, he added, "Let's go." And rolled the dice.

"One," I read aloud.

Lucas rolled his eyes. "That's too easy." As he went to pick it up, I stepped lightly on the back of his hand.

"Na-uh, you didn't say anything about re-rolls. What it is, is what I play. Now, move."

Obediently and with a smirk, Lucas collected the dice and let me have my go. I landed it in three shots and turned to take the few steps back to the start as Lucas lined up his ball. Holding out my hand, he placed the die in my palm, and I jiggled it around slightly before I rolled it out on the turf.

"Five," I said gleefully.

Lucas groaned, though his smirk didn't fade. "This already isn't fair."

"It's your stupid game."

"Hey, *extreme mini-golf* isn't stupid." He located the fifth hole and groaned for dramatic effect when he realized it was further away than six would've been, as it curved under the small stream. "Right. I got this."

He did, in fact, *not* got this, and the ball landed with a *plop* in the water.

"Out!" I cried out as he went to retrieve it. "Maximum shots added."

Smiling, he shook his head. "I'm going to regret introducing you to this game."

By the sixth hole, my sides hurt from laughter, and the staff members were watching us suspiciously as we moved onto the seventh. Lucas took out the second die and rolled them together. "Hah! Ten."

I took a moment to locate the tenth hole. "Shit."

It was decorated with an ornate miniature windmill, but getting to the hole from our position was an impossible shot. The intended trajectory of the ball from hole ten would lead it up a small ramp, which was unreachable from here. Shuffling my feet, I lined up the shot. "I'm going to have to aim for the starting pad of nine, and then go from there."

"It's your play, babe."

The word was uttered with such casualness, and while I'm positive he noticed how my hands gripped the club briefly, I regained myself and smiled at him before I took my shot. However, much like Lucas's shot on hole four, I well overshot, and the ball bounced loudly off the top of the windmill before angling directly toward a teenage couple. The ball had enough momentum to skim the edge of a fake gorilla before it collided with the girl's head. She cried out and fell forward onto her hands and knees, and her boyfriend helped her up before looking around with a glare.

"Hey!" he cried out indignantly.

"Alright, that's it. You two, *out.*" One of the staff members stormed from the small office in the center as menacingly as one can storm when you are forced to step over small gnomes, animal statues, and water features. "No refund, just get out."

It didn't help that both Lucas and I hadn't stopped laughing the entire time, and my shout of, "Sorry!" to the young girl wasn't believed or appreciated as we both burst into another fit of laughter. Lucas grabbed my hand, and we dropped our clubs before we fled the course and back to my car.

Once the doors shut, we descended into another fit of laughter. "So, basically," I started, wiping a stray tear from my cheek. "You work your way through every golf course in the city until you're banned from each one."

"Pretty much." Lucas grinned. "Though the staff turnover is pretty high, especially during the summer. Give it eight months, and you'll be able to go back."

"Good, because I want to play *extreme mini-golf* again."

"I knew it. It's addictive." Our laughter slowed until it died out as we stared at each other, and heat filled the space around us. "Almost as addictive as you," he whispered.

Before I could grasp his words, Lucas leaned forward and pressed his lips to mine. There was no fight for dominance, and I simply opened my mouth and allowed him access. He slid his tongue around the inside of my mouth, exploring every curve and edge, running his tongue along each molar before licking the back of my front teeth.

Chapter Five

Lucas

Tina opened herself to me, her entire body becoming putty in my hands as I deepened the kiss. Reaching up, I caressed her boobies through her top, and her nipples twitched as though they were mice sniffing the air for predators. But the only predator around here was the one in my pants, ready to soak them in my custard.

A pants predator.

A *pantador*, if you will.

As I teased the underneath of her tongue with mine, making it squirt saliva into my waiting mouth, I couldn't contain my moan, and pulled her top up to expose her heavy milk duds. I palmed them, twisting and touching as though I were tuning a radio, and pulled away only enough to whisper against her lips, "You're so fucking beautiful, when can I see you again?"

Tina put her hands on my shoulders, and reluctantly, I pulled back. Her expression had changed, and my brow dipped down even as I panted through the desire that still pumped around my body.

"Lucas," she breathed my name out, and my expression shifted as I picked up on the different energy in the car. Something had changed, and for the life of me, I couldn't figure out what it was. Within seconds, it had gone from hot-and-bothered to cold-and-clammy. She pulled her t-shirt down over her breasts. Gravity had no meaning for such glorious juggernauts, and I couldn't stop staring at them. They bounced of their own volition, jiggling even when there was no breeze present in the car. Tina scratched at one, and it caused a cascade of motion, rippling and undulating like an ocean I wanted to dive into.

"Lucas," Tina repeated my name as the fabric entirely hid her lady lumps from my view. "We need to talk."

I stilled.

We need to talk.

Nothing good ever followed those words, and before Tina had even said anything further, I shrank against the door of the car and watched her wearily. We'd had a good time, no, a *great* time. We'd done nothing but laugh for the past hour. Being with Tina was like having that first crush as a teenager all over again. The energy between us was electric, and high off that energy, I'd kissed her, and Tina had melted into the kiss.

Until she hadn't.

Dropping my head to my chest, I thought I already understood what she was going to say before she said it. Tina didn't *do* relationships, and despite the fun we'd had, that's all this had been to her.

Fun.

"Lucas," the third time she repeated my name, and all previous passion had vanished from the word. I found I didn't want to hear it.

"It's okay," I started, holding up a hand. "I know what you're going to say."

Her eyebrows shot up and disappeared into her hairline. "You do?"

"Yes. You're going to tell me that you don't want a relationship, that this is all moving too fast, and what started as a little fun has already gone too far.

You're going to say you had a lot of fun today, but this is where it ends." When I raised my eyes to hers, her orbs were wide and shimmering with a hint of tears. A stab of anger moved through my organs. Why is *she* crying? She's the one ending it before it even had a chance to be anything.

"That's right," she said quietly.

I nodded. I knew, of course, I knew. I knew from the moment she'd led me to that bathroom yesterday. Tina wasn't looking for anything beyond a bit of horizontal refreshment in the form of some rigorous beard-splitting.

No matter what I had tried to convince myself of last night, how I told myself if that's all she wanted, then I was willing to provide it... I couldn't do it. Every moment I spent with her shifted something further inside me, and feelings were developing despite us barely knowing each other. If that frightened Tina, I could understand, but she wanted to shut it down before it even had the chance to bloom as her beautiful snatch bloomed for me last night.

"I understand," I said, and looked at my hands, still warm from the heavy weight of her bazoongas, which had rested in my palms only minutes before. My gaze fell to her chubby chest cheeks again, now hidden behind her t-shirt, and her nipples quivered sadly as though they, too, missed my touch. "I'll catch a cab home."

When I moved to open the door, Tina reached across the space between us, and her hand landed on my leg. "Wait, Lucas, you don't have to leave."

"It's better this way," I said, and touched my hand on top of hers briefly before pushing it away. "It's okay, really." I tried to smile but failed. "You're allowed to want, and not want, what is right for you. I knew last night you didn't want something more, but I stayed because... well, anyway. It was lovely spending time with you, Tina. Bye."

Before she could say anything further, I slipped out of the car and closed the door behind me. Shoving my hands in my pockets, I walked purposefully toward the main road, ready to hail down the first cab I saw. Despite my life not being a romance movie, the clouds had started to gather, blocking out the sun and dimming the light that had shone so brightly when I was with Tina.

In my pants, my pink cigar and brovaries drooped sadly.

Chapter Six

Tina

If Lily weren't already suspicious when I was the one to call her, when usually it was the other way around, then she was *certainly* suspicious when I asked her if she wanted to grab lunch. It had been a week since I'd seen or heard from Lucas, and work had been hell. I hadn't been able to concentrate on a damn thing, and the usual Monday to Friday had dragged more than ever. The time between the phone ringing while on reception was filled with silence in my mind that the dull drone of the radio couldn't cover. Usually, I'd be thinking of the weekend, nights out with the girls, or nights in with myself. Maybe I'd even think about day-to-day things like bills that needed to be paid, but there was never the dull white noise that seemed to fill my brain this week.

Except when I thought of Lucas, then the white noise stopped, and I found myself smiling like an idiot.

I *was* an idiot.

Not only had I let him go, but I'd straight-up pushed him away. Lucas had read me like an open book, and although it appeared he had been expecting me to do exactly as I did, the hurt which radiated from his kale-green eyes stuck in my mind.

For the first time in a long time, I didn't feel like calling my friends. I didn't want a night out or drinks, and the first person who popped into my mind, other than Lucas, obviously, was Lily. She wanted to spend more time with me, and I always felt bad that we didn't. But we were completely different people, and wanted different things from life.

Or so I thought.

Lily watched me carefully as she slid into the white chair opposite me. We'd chosen a local café with a stunning outdoor area, which was popular for its brunches. The brunch crowd was filing out, and there were many empty tables, so Lily and I were able to have a conversation and enjoy the sunshine. Small groups of people still hovered around the outskirts of the area, closer to the edge of the balcony that overlooked the garden, and their semi-drunken laughter rose above the general chatter now and then.

"This is unexpected," she said as she tucked her

purse under her leg. There was no judgment in her tone, but her fluid-filled spheres softened as she looked at me. It stung a bit that she thought the only reason I'd ever call her was when something was wrong.

But what stung even more was that it was the truth.

Damn, I need to try harder.

"I know," I said finally, and rubbed my arm absentmindedly. "I'm sorry, we really should catch up more often…" After a pause, I added, "What are the boys up to today?"

Lily smiled, that smile she got whenever she thought of her son and husband. "Ernie is going to take Evan to the beach."

I balked. "To the beach? I know the sun is out, but the water will be *freezing.*"

Lily shrugged with one shoulder, still grinning. "Yeah, but they're boys, and boys are…"

"Stupid?"

"Yes." She laughed.

The waiter appeared, and we ordered. After he'd brought a bottle of water and two glasses, Lily watched me quietly as I poured us both a drink.

Finally, she said, "Do you need to talk about something?"

I paused, and didn't regain myself quickly enough for it to be unnoticeable. "No."

Her smile was soft. "Liar."

"Okay." I placed the bottle down on the table and leaned forward, resting my chin in my palms. "I do, but I don't want to. Not right now."

Her eyes narrowed. "I'll accept that, but only for the moment. If you need to talk, you need to talk. It's not good to bottle things up."

"I know."

Lily's lips curved into a smile. "How about this? There's something I've been meaning to ask you, and it'll *definitely* distract you from..." She waved her hand between us. "Whatever is going on with you."

I tilted my head. "I'm intrigued, tell me more."

All at once, her cheeks flushed pink, and Lily took a hurried gulp of the cool water before sighing. "It's kind of embarrassing." As I leaned further forward, Lily laughed nervously. "You're *so keen* for me to embarrass myself."

I raised a hand. "I promise I won't judge."

"Okay." She took a deep breath and eyed me suspiciously for a moment before continuing, "You know Ernie and I have been together a long time."

"Yes..."

"And I wanted to ask you..." Lily cleared her throat and took another sip of water. "For some pointers on..."

"Slurping the love whistle?"

"Oh my God." Lily covered her eyes with her fingers before dropping her hands to the table with a slap. "Yes. That."

"But surely you've gone bagpiping before?"

"Of *course,* I have. But I wanted to maybe try something new. Blow his mind."

I released an impressed *harrumph* and couldn't help but smile. "Well, I hope he's returning the favor."

Lily's cheeks reddened again. "Yes, he does."

"Alright then. Anything in particular you want–"

"Just… give me some ideas. Tell me what you do."

My grin widened. I *loved* that Lily was coming to me with this. We rarely spoke about sex, despite it being one of my favorite topics. I always assumed she silently judged me for my free lifestyle, but perhaps that was only an assumption on my part. Here she was, having an open conversation, and, while her discomfort was evident, it was still so cool that she'd asked *me* rather than trying some internet forum searches or something.

"Okay." I glanced around for dramatic effect, and Lily's eyes widened as she followed suit. I laughed. "Relax, this place is near empty, and they can't hear anything from there." I indicated the tipsy group on the other side of the balcony. "Okay, first thing you want to do is grab that doodle with both hands. Lower your lips to it and... *smack* yourself across the face with it."

Lily recoiled. "What?"

"Do it hard, hard enough to make a satisfying sound."

"And guys like that?"

"They love it. Then, do the same thing on your tongue."

Lily nodded, though she was looking more uncertain by the minute.

Gleefully, I continued. "Gargle those balls, gargle them *hard*. Make as much noise as possible, like you've filled your mouth with a ladleful of jam and are sloshing it around with his plums."

"Oh, my..." Lily's cheeks remained pinkened as she took another sip of water.

"Here, do this." I smacked my tongue against the inside of my bottom lip. "Hear that?" Lily nodded and tried to copy the sound without actually making it. "That's what you're going for. Get a good squelchy symphony going."

Lily laughed nervously as I paused long enough for our lunch to be served, and she looked at the table until the waiter had moved away.

"And if you really want to blow his mind," I continued as I picked up my fork. "Stick a finger in his dookie-chute."

The clatter of Lily's fork hitting the plate sounded loud enough to draw the attention of the other dining group, and she scrambled to pick it up. "Are you serious?" she hissed out at me as she leaned forward.

"Sure, I am. Don't just go for it, though, you gotta rub it a bit first, dirty talk to him about it. But I promise, he'll love it."

"You are too much," Lily whispered through a smile.

"Does that help?"

"You've uh, given me a lot to work with."

"That's Ernie's job."

"Oh my God, *Tina.*" Lily swiped a hand half-heartedly toward me, and I laughed.

Lunch was relaxed, and we enjoyed our meals at a leisurely pace while chatting. Lily told me about how Evan was doing at school, Ernie's recent promotion, and the renovations they wanted to do to the house. I told her about my work—there wasn't much to tell—but mostly listened, and specifically avoided the one topic I *should* have been discussing.

Lucas.

"Hey there."

I looked up as a man approached our table, and before waiting for an answer, he pulled up a chair and sat next to me, staring at me and wiggling his eyebrows. Lily smirked and continued eating as she watched me.

"Hi," I said.

"I noticed you from over there." He indicated the tipsy group with his thumb. "Do you believe in love at first sight, or should I walk past again?"

I smiled. "Thank you, but I'm not interested."

"That's a pity, because you remind me of my little toe."

"I'm sorry?"

"Because I'll probably bang you against the dining table when I'm drunk."

"Listen–" I started.

"Your panties must be a mirror, because I can see myself in them."

"Hey." I placed a finger on his lips, and he eyed me seductively and pursed his pillow lips. "This is all very charming, but I'm not interested. Okay?"

His eyebrows drooped with his expression, and he grabbed my wrist and kissed the inside of my palm before moving my hand away. "That's a pity, you're so beautiful I'd suck your Dad's cock just to taste the recipe that made you. I just... I want to sex you up so fucking hard."

Something fluttered inside me, but I restrained myself. "I'm sorry."

He pressed his lips together in an imitation of a smile and moved away.

"Wow," Lily said.

"What?"

"It's just... he said all the right things, he was handsome, and I *know* you've got a thing for eyebrows. I didn't expect you to turn him down."

"Just not in the mood, I guess."

"That magician got under your skin pretty hard, huh?"

My gaze shot up to meet Lily's. "What?"

Lily rolled her eyes. "Don't think I didn't notice you two sneak off last week, and you did tell me you'd be seeing him later that night. Then a week later, you call me out of the blue for lunch, down in the dumps, and refusing to talk? It doesn't take a genius to put two and two together, Tina."

I rubbed my face. "That obvious, huh?"

"To me it is." Lily waited until I met her gaze again. "I know we're different people, but we're sisters, and I *know* you. But I don't think I've ever seen you smitten before."

"I'm not smitten."

Lily scoffed, though she still smiled. "Look into my eyes, and say that again."

I met her orby orbs with my own, and as I opened my mouth to answer, the waiter reappeared with our desserts. As he set down my custard slice, the plate tilted, and it oozed slightly to the side with a slick schloop.

I smiled to myself as my thoughts shifted once again to Lucas, before my smile dropped. "You're right, I am smitten. I can't stop thinking about him."

"So, what are you waiting for?"

I shook my head. "I hurt him."

"He'll forgive you."

"You can't know that for sure."

She placed a hand over mine. "He'll forgive you."

Lily looked so certain, and I tried to conjure

some of the certainty myself.

Chapter Seven

Lucas

The quiet days during the week between shows were usually something I relished, but this past week, every moment of silence was agony. I should never have allowed myself to hope for a future with Tina, because it was clear from the start that she was only in it for the fun. Her wants and needs were fine, but even though I had known, I'd allowed my feelings to get involved, and to trick myself into believing it might be the same for her.

A Sunday afternoon magic show was my saving grace, and I plastered on a smile and put on the best damn show I could, laughing and engaging. The kids' laughter eased the tension in my chest, but it never fully left.

As I was packing up, I felt a presence behind me, but before I worked up the energy to turn and engage with whoever it was, I took a few deep breaths. It was too much to hope it was Tina, though the sensation was so similar to a week ago when she'd first approached me, it brought a pang to my chest.

"So, have you been doing magic long?"

My hands stilled, and I dropped the props I held into the box before me. Turning, I found Tina, her face lit with a nervous and entirely unconvincing smile.

My brow furrowed. "How did you know where I'd be?" The party was in a public park, but it was still a stretch this was a coincidence.

Her smile dropped before she worked to replace it with one equally as strained. "Lily made a call to the agency, said you'd left something at her place, and she wanted to return it. They told us where to find you."

"I'll remember that method if I ever want to murder one of my co-workers."

Tina's expression shifted as though she didn't know whether she should laugh or not. My mind was still reeling at the fact that she was here in front of me, and my attempt to break the ice had fallen short.

Tina fidgeted on the spot slightly and eventually murmured, "I've been thinking about you."

"What?"

"Here," she said as she shoved her cell in front of my face. I watched the video as it unfolded—a hamster running on a wheel, its ballsack slapping about.

I couldn't help myself. I burst out laughing. "What the fuck, Tina?"

She lifted a shoulder. "I thought if I couldn't break the ice, then a slapping hamster ballsack might do it for me." Tina paused and huffed out a laugh. "There's a sentence I never thought I'd say."

My grin faded as I watched her face. "What are you doing here?"

She rubbed her arm. "Look, I'm not good at this, so I'm just going to say it. I miss you. I like you... a *lot*. I haven't been able to stop thinking about you all week. I know I hurt you, and I'm sorry, but if you can find it in yourself to give me a second chance, I'd like to... date you and stuff."

"It's the *and stuff* part I'm interested in."

Tina slapped my arm gently as she laughed. "Oh, shut up."

"Ah, but it made you smile."

Her eyes met mine, and the shift in her face was evident when the smile was genuine. I returned her smile and clasped her hand in mine. Tina watched the movement with wide eyes, as though it were something new to her.

"I forgive you, and I'd love to date you," I said, because it *was* that easy. We were on different pages when we met, but her coming here to find me and tell me how she felt changed everything. I felt it too, and I wasn't going to drag myself or the possibility of an *us* down by lingering on what was nothing more than a misunderstanding. "If you help me pack up, we can be back at mine in forty minutes."

Her eyes lit up with promise. "Deal."

We barely made it through the door of my place

before we were on each other. My props from the show I'd left in the car, and as Tina pulled up behind me in the driveway, we practically ran to the house. Before the door had even closed with a quiet click, her tongue was in my mouth, swirling around mine in a game where the goal was to taste as much of each other as possible.

"You taste like sprinkles," she said breathlessly as she pulled away, moving back only enough to talk so I could still feel the warmth of her breath against my lips.

"I can't wait to taste your liquid silk on my tongue."

Tina moaned and plummeted her tongue back into my mouth. The sounds we made were sweet suction as we plunged each other's faces, both of us equally as desperate to get as much of the other as possible. With a gasp, Tina stepped back, and while holding my eye contact, pulled her t-shirt over her head and discarded it. Again, I was enraptured by the mesmerizing sway of her flesh bongos. My gaze found hers as she kicked off her shoes and removed one sock, then another. Then another sock, and another, and another, and another.

"My feet get cold," she purred with a grin.

"I'll make sure you're all warmed up, baby," I said, rubbing myself through my pants. "I'll nibble those sweaty toe pads."

Tina's cheeks were flushed with desire as she removed her jeans next. I couldn't take it any longer and closed the gap between us. Tracing my fingers down her stomach, I pushed my hand behind the barrier of her panties. She was already soaked for me, her bearded clam snapping playfully away at my fingers as I ran my digits through her spendings. She opened her mouth as if she was going to say something, but the words died on her lips and turned into a moan as I shoved two fingers inside her cooter.

Her legs trembled as I fingered her hard and fast, pumping into her squeeze box as it lived up to its name and squeezed around the intrusion. But I was on a mission, and added a third finger into the sloppy goodness of her slit and moved faster.

"Oh, *God*, Lucas!" Tina cried out, gripping my shoulders and throwing her head back.

Finally, I got what I wanted, and a delightful queef squeezed past her flaps. Groaning, I kept going, making her flange sing for me. Her slop hole and flaps made music in unison as her fanny juice leaked down my hand.

"There she is," I whispered, nipping at her ear. "There's the loose balloon I fell for."

Tina moaned and tilted her head to the side to give me access to her neck, and I left a snail-trail of saliva as I licked from her ear to her collarbone.

"Please, I need your willymilk inside me."

"Gonna fill you up. Gonna get you pregnant with my wormgob so you can fart a baby out your vagina."

Tina groaned and grabbed my knob through my pants before she rushed to undo the buttons. Not soon enough, we were both naked and kissing wildly, our tongues tornadoing around each other as we made our way into the bedroom. Tina fell backward onto the mattress, bouncing slightly as I crawled over her.

"Now. *Now.* Please," she begged.

Who was I to deny this goddess?

Plunging into her, I shifted my gearstick into full throttle and drove into her hard. Tina cried out, and I fiddled with my dangling plumbs and pulled into reverse, only to jump straight into third gear and thrust hard into her again. My pounding was unforgiving, and Tina gripped my arms with her nails as she cried out in mind-bending pleasure, her nether regions gripping and flexing around me so deliciously. Giving it to her hard, her gelatinous bosom jiggled with the motion. Each jiggle continued after the thrust had ended, and I did it again, and again, wanting the jiggling waves of her twins to double up on itself. Like when you're taking a bath and slide back and forth over and over until you create a mini tidal wave, I wanted the ripple of her flesh to jump over itself and make her gasp. I wanted them to jiggle so hard from the masculine power of my beating of her guts that her tatas leapt up and slapped her in the face in joy.

"God," Tina panted out, taking everything I had to give her. "You're so good. Can you forgive me for hurting you?"

"I already forgave you," I replied, and planted a kiss on her lips, our mouths sliding over each other like two fish dancing in seaweed-infested water. "Now lie back and enjoy the assault with my pleasure weapon, because I'm about to fill you with my cock snot."

Chapter Eight

TINA

Lucas stood behind me, and a tremble ran through my body at his presence. We were meant to be getting ready for lunch with Lily and her family for Evan's seventh birthday, but it was difficult not to get distracted when I had the sexiest man on Earth living with me.

He growled loudly next to my ear, his lips rolling sensually over each other and against my neck. Lucas's hands landed on my ass and squeezed, and before I could say anything, he pushed me forward toward the mattress, and I landed on all fours.

Arching my back and naked from the waist down, I looked over my shoulder as he eyed my slit. His brow furrowed, and he kneeled before tonguing at my flaps. Flicking his finger between them, he played with the string of my tampon.

"Does this mean there's no fun-time when we get back?"

I smirked at him and wiggled my hips. "Not necessarily."

He tugged lightly at the string, and I gasped as an explosion of pleasure shifted through me at the movement inside my channel. So sensitive was my love tunnel whenever Lucas was near me. "If I were a vampire, I could use this as a teabag."

Sighing, I smiled. "How did I get so lucky to land someone so romantic?"

"Don't speak too soon," he warned as he rubbed

at my pleasure bean and reached down with the other hand to work himself. "I'm thinking all sorts of dirty thoughts."

"Lucas–"

"Surely we have time for me to get my girl off?" His magic fingers were doing their job, opening up my petals and unfurling my coochie so he could rub at my button, and he chuckled as I moaned. "Maybe I'll give your cherry pie a rest while you're riding the red dragon. Maybe I'll explore this instead..."

I gasped as he traced his finger up and rubbed against my brownie bowl.

"What do you think of that, huh? Maybe I'll fill your turd blower with the fizz of my jizz stick?"

I couldn't speak as he pushed a finger inside my chocolate pocket and worked it in and out slowly. My head dropped to the mattress as he continued to rub himself, and leaned forward to tongue-punch the bud of my pleasure. My moans drove him forward, and I felt the vibrations of his own against my honey pot.

"Watch out," he mumbled between licks. "There's a tornado warning. Gonna make a swirly wirly of my orgasm goop on you."

"Please, I want to swallow it."

He groaned loudly as he licked me faster, and my rear ring tightened around his finger as I came.

"Fuck, Tina, you're too much," Lucas said as he stood, and I dropped to my knees next to the bed and opened my mouth. "Keep that mouth open, gonna sandblast your teeth with my blue-veined custard chucker."

My vag tingled in post-orgasm bliss as I watched him work himself, and his crotch nuggets twitched as he neared his peak.

"Give it to me, baby," I whispered, and wiggled my tongue at him. "Coat my mouth in your daddy sauce."

Lucas moaned as his member hardened further, the head turning pink, throbbing, and swelling before he released on my face. I opened my mouth and hummed as load after load of his ball barf landed on my tongue. He dropped to his knees next to me and rested his forehead against mine as I slurped up the last of his dongwater from my chin and lips.

"I'm so lucky to have you," he whispered between pants, and I licked his cheek and giggled.

"I'm lucky to have you."

His green-bean eyes opened and stared me down, and a wicked grin spread across his lips. "We're going to be late."

"And whose fault is that?"

His laugh filled my chest with warmth. "I look forward to ploughing that rusty bunghole later." A tremble moved through my body again, and I clenched my thighs. Lucas laughed again before he moved to stand and held a hand out for me. "Are you going to wear those shorts I like?"

"But they give me camel-toe," I argued.

He grinned, and his eyebrow undulated in a way he knew I couldn't possibly resist. "That's why I like them. Maybe I'll wear shorts too, and your camel-toe can play with my moose-knuckle."

I sighed, and my smile dropped as I stared into his orbs with my orbs. Just four orbs watching each other romantically. "You know I love you, right?"

Lucas's smile softened, but didn't disappear. "I love you too, babe."

And not for the first time, I was thankful his magic hands had caught my eye.

Acknowledgements

There are three main parties I need to thank for Abraca-Doodle, whether they want to take responsibility or not.

Firstly, and always with every book, my wonderful partner, Jason. He's incredibly supportive of my author journey, but aside from that, and in regard to Abraca-Doodle in particular, several of the terminologies used are his. We share a sense of humor and will sit there thinking of the worst terms we can, and they'll always make it into the book.

If not this one, then the next one... yeah, there'll be more. The doodle-verse has opened up in my mind now, and apparently, there's no going back, so let's embrace it in all its cringey glory.

Secondly, my wonderful circle of friends, who not only wholeheartedly encouraged me to embrace my oddness when I mentioned I wanted to try to be more my authentic self, but would send me any memes or reels of anything cringe. So, I thank them for their ongoing support, even if the WIP snippets I sent them scarred them for life.

And last, but definitely not least, I need to thank the readers. Doodle Me was written as a bit of fun for myself. It was something I used as a palate cleanser between writing darker romances, and originally, I didn't intend to publish it. When it was finished, I figured, what the hey, and put it out there in the world. The response blew me away. I genuinely wasn't expecting to find this incredible reader base who absolutely lapped up the gooey goodness of the humor in Doodle Me, and who cried out for more like the little naughty turnips you are.

Abraca-Doodle is, I'd say, more unhinged than Doodle Me. Because I took the vibe and leaned into it, *hard*. So, if this book made you cringe harder than Doodle Me did, if you had to put it down and stare at the wall and listen to the elevator music in your head while your brain tried to comprehend what the fuck you just read... really, you only have yourself to blame for encouraging me.

But in all seriousness, thank you. It's been a blast, and I will continue to bring the weird under Eva Everhard.

As always, if you loved it, leave a review. We authors are delicate creatures, and we sit in the dark with wild eyes, cupping our coffee and a fluffy blanket, waiting to hear if our readers loved our work.

Love to all x

Eva Everhard is a sarcastic, slightly unhinged, Aussie author who cackles manically over her latest and greatest piece of literature, chock full of cringeworthy slang that will make you laugh or vomit.
Maybe a little of both at the same time.

Her books are so spicy you'll wonder what took you so long to read them, while also questioning every decision you've made that led you to this moment.

Eva's mind is bursting with doodles, and she can't wait to unleash her new goal on her readers—become more unhinged.

To the English Teacher who said my stories were too dramatic—look at me now!

You can stay up to date with Eva and her alter ego at www.angelsandfirebooks.com.au

www.ingramcontent.com/pod-product-compliance
Lightning Source LLC
LaVergne TN
LVHW091556060526
838200LV00036B/871